MEET ALL THESE FRIENDS IN BUZZ BOOKS:

Thomas the Tank Engine
The Animals of Farthing Wood
Biker Mice From Mars
James Bond Junior
Fireman Sam
Joshua Jones
Rupert
Babar

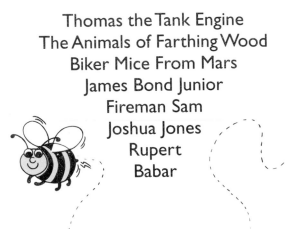

First published in Great Britain 1994 by Buzz Books,
an imprint of Reed Children's Books
Michelin House, 81 Fulham Road, London SW3 6RB
and Auckland, Melbourne, Singapore and Toronto

The Animals of Farthing Wood © copyright 1979 Colin Dann
Storylines © copyright European Broadcasting Union 1992
Text © copyright 1994 Reed International Books Limited
Illustrations © copyright 1994 Reed International Books Limited
Based on the novels by Colin Dann and the animation series
produced by Telemagination and La Fabrique for the BBC
and the European Broadcasting Union.
All rights reserved.

ISBN 1 85591 447 6

Printed in Italy by Olivotto

Trouble in the Park

Story by Colin Dann
Text by Mary Risk
Illustrations by The County Studio

buzz books

By the springtime, many of the Farthing Wood animals had found mates in White Deer Park, and their young were growing up around them.

But danger still threatened. Scarface, the blue fox, was their bitter enemy.

6

"My baby! He's eaten one of my babies!"
sobbed Father Rabbit one day to Fox.

"We'll have no peace until we deal with
that vicious blue fox!" said Fox angrily.

"Adder can do it," cackled Weasel.

"Hmm," said Fox. "Weasel, ask Adder to
give the blue foxes a bit of a scare."

Weasel was gone before Fox had finished.

Weasel and her mate, Measly, found
Adder under a stone. Adder uncoiled
herself and started to slither away.

"Adder, come back!" yelled Weasel.
"I've got a message for you from Fox."

"Yes," said Measly, "he said — "

"He wants you to deal with a blue fox,"
finished Weasel.

"I sssee," hissed Adder. "Which one?"

"Any one will do," said Weasel. "Just
deal with it. We must have some peace."

"I shall enjoy thisss," hissed Adder.

Not all of the blue foxes wanted war. Ranger, Scarface's son, had something quite different on his mind. He spotted Fox's daughter, Charmer, as she bent gracefully to drink at the stream.

"She's lovely!" he thought.

He stepped closer. Just then, Charmer looked up.

"Go away!" she said. "This is our land."

"I don't want to hurt you," said Ranger.
"I want to be your friend."

"But you're Scarface's son," said Charmer.
"He's my father's enemy."

"But why can't you and I be friends?"
said Ranger. "Can I see you again?"

"Maybe," said Charmer, and she ran away.

"It'sss time thossse blue foxesss learnt a
lessson," thought Adder. She coiled
herself up, ready to attack.

She waited for a long time. At last,
Bounder, Ranger's brother, came down
the path. He'd enjoyed his portion of the
baby rabbit. Suddenly, Adder struck.
Bounder fell over, and lay still.

12

From overhead, Whistler was watching.

"Adder's bitten the wrong fox!" he said, flapping down to land by Fox's earth. "It wasn't Scarface!"

"Oh no!" said Fox. "The weasels must have got mixed up when they spoke to Adder. Now Scarface will want revenge!"

"You silly pair of weasels," said Kestrel.
"You gave Adder the wrong message, and
now we'll all be in trouble."

"You're hopeless," Owl hooted.

"We want justice!" shrieked Weasel.

"Very well," said Owl. "You shall have a trial, and I'll be the judge."

"Oh," said Weasel. "I've changed my mind!" and she began to run away.

"Guard them, Kestrel," said Owl.

"The Farthing Wood Fox did this!" stormed Scarface when he saw his dead son.

"It can't have been Fox, Father," said Ranger quickly. "It's a snake bite. Look."

"My poor Bounder," shuddered Lady Blue. "I'll bet it was the Farthing Wood snake."

"You're right," said Scarface slowly.
"And Fox put her up to it. I'll get that
snake first, then it's Fox's turn."

He loped away towards Adder's rock.

"Oh no!" thought Ranger. "When will
this quarrel ever end?"

The Farthing Wood animals were jittery.

"The wrong fox?" chattered the squirrels. "Oh, dear!"

"Don't panic!" said Mother Rabbit.

"Why not?" moaned Father Rabbit.

"If I were you, Adder," said Owl, "I'd lie low. Scarface must be furious."

"Lie low? Sssilly Owl. How can I get any lower?" snapped Adder.

That afternoon, Adder wriggled under her
stone. She wriggled in as far as she could,
but the tip of her tail was still showing.
Scarface spotted her. With a tap of his
paw, he pushed the stone away.

"Gotcha!" said Scarface, pouncing.
"Not quite," said Adder, darting away.
But Scarface moved like lightning. He
caught Adder in his paw and threw her
into the air. Adder crashed to the ground.

Scarface crouched to jump again, but
Adder quickly wriggled into a hole in the
dirt. She wasn't quick enough. Scarface's
teeth closed on the tip of her tail. She
thrashed about desperately. Suddenly,
she was free.

"You ssscoundrel!" she hissed. "You've
bitten off my tail!"

Everything was ready for the weasels' trial. Owl was the judge, Kestrel was the clerk and the squirrels, rabbits and mice had come to watch.

"I confess!" smirked Measly. "Weasel gave Adder the wrong message!"

"You can't confess for anyone else," said Owl sternly. "I sentence you both to a dipping in the pond."

The squirrels and rabbits burst out laughing as the weasels hit the water with a splash.

Not everyone was out in the spring
sunshine. Underground, old Badger lay
dreaming of days long ago, and his old
friend Mole.

"Moley? Is that you?" he murmured.

It was Mossy, Mole's son. "Badger, are
you all right?" he whispered.

"Oh, yes," said Badger. "How good it is
here, in my old set in Farthing Wood..."

"But this isn't..." began Mossy.

"...I'm going to sleep now, Moley, for a
long, long time..."

"Oh Badger! Dear Badger!" sobbed Mossy,
and he ran off to find Fox.

Fox and Vixen came at once.

"Badger, it's me," said Fox.

Vixen nudged him gently with her nose.

"Come to persuade me to leave Farthing Wood, have you Fox?" said Badger. "I won't go. I'll stay here, forever."

"So you shall, old friend," said Fox, as Badger shut his eyes for the last time.

Outside the set, the Farthing Wood
animals stood quietly, waiting for news.
When they saw the sadness on Fox's face,
they knew that Badger had died.

"He was a wise, brave animal, and a true
and faithful friend," said Fox.

The Farthing Wood animals had lost one of their dearest friends.

"The death of a loved one is never easy," Fox said to Vixen. "I do feel sorry for Scarface and Lady Blue for losing Bounder. Remember how we felt when we lost our Dreamer."

"Yes," Vixen agreed. "How I wish Scarface had never started this feud." She looked at Fox, her eyes clouded with sadness.

"If we all protect each other, we'll be safe," said Fox.

But he was worried, too.